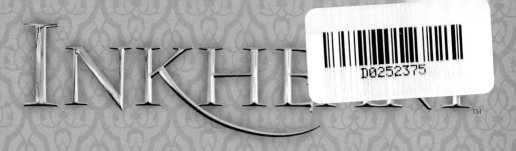

FARID'S STORY

Adapted by Gail Herman
From the screenplay written by David Lindsay-Abaire
Based on the novel by Cornelia Funke

SCHOLASTIC INC.

New York   Toronto   London   Auckland   Sydney
Mexico City   New Delhi   Hong Kong   Buenos Aires

ISBN-10: 0-545-00710-0
ISBN-13: 978-0-545-00710-8

Published by Scholastic Inc.
SCHOLASTIC and associated logos are trademarks and/or registered trademarks of Scholastic Inc.

12 11 10 9 8 7 6 5 4 3 2 1   9 10 11 12/0

Printed in the U.S.A.
First printing, January 2009

One minute, Farid was where he should
be, in the desert with a gang of thieves.
The next minute, the desert was gone.
Farid was in a castle.
Men in black jackets stood around him.

"Put the boy in the stables!"
cried the leader of the men.
His name was Capricorn.

Farid was alone and scared.

More people were put in the stables: a girl named Meggie, her dad Mo, and her aunt Elinor.

Farid listened as they spoke and learned the truth.

Mo had a gift.
When he read aloud,
people and things came out of books.
Farid came out of one.
So did Capricorn and the men in
black jackets.
They were from a story called *Inkheart*.

But for every person who came out of
a book, another one went inside.
Resa, Meggie's mom, had gone into *Inkheart*.
Mo had to get her out.
He needed to find another copy of the book,
since Capricorn had destroyed his.
"Let's find the author to get another one!"
said Meggie.

Dustfinger was also from *Inkheart*.
He wanted to get the book, too.
He needed to go back inside,
back to his family.
He needed Mo's help.
But Mo was locked in the stable.

Dustfinger had an idea . . .
He gave Mo a copy of
The Wonderful Wizard of Oz.
Mo began to read.
He read about the tornado.
Soon wind howled around the castle.
Then the walls of the stable crumbled.
They were free!

Farid stayed close to the
others as they ran.

Farid was free, but he was confused.
Everything was so different.
In his own world, he had a hard life
with no friends or family.
Maybe things here could be better.

Farid was given new clothes.
While Mo and Meggie went to look
for the author, he and Dustfinger went
to the town square. Musicians played.
Magicians performed.

But none of them could match
Dustfinger's tricks. Dustfinger
snapped his fingers.
Flames danced at his fingertips.
Fire streamed from his mouth.
"Teach me these magic tricks!"
Farid begged.

Farid liked this new world.
"No slave drivers!" he said.
"No sandstorms! No fleas!"
And he was happy to have
some friends.

Mo and Dustfinger found the author
of *Inkheart*.
His name was Fenoglio.
He gave them the pages of the book.
Then Dustfinger told Mo a secret.

Resa had already been read out of the
book by someone else. She was a prisoner
at Capricorn's castle.

Mo had to get to the castle to find her. He and Dustfinger took Fenoglio's car. They didn't know that Farid was hiding in the trunk.

When Dustfinger found Farid
in the trunk, he was angry.

But it was too late to send Farid back.
He'd have to come with them.

Mo, Dustfinger, and Farid snuck
back into the castle.

Mo went to find Resa while
Dustfinger and Farid stood watch.
Farid practiced magic tricks.
Suddenly they saw the Black Jackets.

Dustfinger was caught,
but Farid was clever.
He escaped.
Then he tricked the guard
and freed Dustfinger.

Meanwhile Meggie and Fenoglio
had been taken by the Black Jackets
back to Capricorn's castle.
Capricorn had a plan for them.

Resa and Fenoglio were put into a cage.
Capricorn had saved one copy of *Inkheart*.
And he was forcing Meggie to read it aloud.

Like Mo, Meggie could read
things out of books.
Now Capricorn wanted her to
read out The Shadow,
the book's most deadly creature.
But Meggie had a different plan.

Meggie began to write her own story.
She wrote on her arm and her legs.
And she read aloud as she wrote.
" 'The Shadow and his master blew away
like ashes in the wind.' "
Capricorn and The Shadow disappeared.
The Black Jackets disappeared, too!

But Dustfinger and Farid were too late.
"I missed it!" Dustfinger shouted.
"Everyone went back but me."
Angry, Dustfinger raced away.

Farid hurried after Dustfinger.
"If you are leaving," Farid said,
"at least take this."
He held out the last copy of *Inkheart*.
"You stole it for me!" Dustfinger cried.
Farid grinned.

Then Mo appeared.
He wanted to help Dustfinger get home.
So he picked up the book and began to
read. Suddenly, Dustfinger disappeared!
It had worked! Mo had read him back
into the book.

Farid was sad that his friend was gone,
but at least he had Meggie, Mo, and Resa.
Together they could form a family.
Farid finally felt like he belonged.